Easter Mice!

Easter Mice!

BY BETHANY ROBERTS

ILLUSTRATED BY DOUG CUSHMAN

Green Light Readers
HOUGHTON MIFFLIN HARCOURT
Boston   New York

www.hmhco.com

The Library of Congress has cataloged the hardcover edition as follows:
Roberts, Bethany.
Easter mice! / by Bethany Roberts; illustrated by Doug Cushman.
p. cm.
Summary: Four mice enjoy a beautiful spring day as they hunt for Easter eggs.
[1. Easter—Fiction. 2. Mice—Fiction. 3. Eggs—Fiction. 4. Easter eggs—Fiction.
5. Stories in rhyme.]
I. Cushman, Doug, ill. II. Title
PZ8.3.R5295 Eas 2003
[E]—dc21
2002007973

ISBN: 978-0-618-16455-4 hardcover
ISBN: 978-0-544-55543-3 GLR paperback
ISBN: 978-0-544-55544-0 GLR paper over board

Manufactured in China
SCP 10 9 8 7 6 5 4 3 2 1

4500557321

Happy Easter to Bob, Krista, and Melissa
—B.R.

To my friends at Sot-l'y-Laisse
—D.C.

Easter mice
hop, hop, hop!

Time for the egg hunt.
Who will win?

Easter mice
jump, jump, jump!
Ready, set, let's begin!

Look, look
around the tulips.
One egg, two eggs, three eggs, four!

Peek, peek
behind the daffodils.

Spotted eggs, striped eggs!
More, more, more!

One little mouse
picking flowers.

Sniff! Whiff!
Spring! Fling!

Mud pies, mud feet,
wiggle like a worm.

Laugh with a ladybug,
swing, swing, swing!

Ride, glide,
boating in a puddle.

One little mouse
falls in. Splash!

Leapfrog, leapfrog,
bounce, bounce, bounce.

Race with a robin,
dash, dash, dash!

Stop the egg hunt!
Count! Let's see—

which little mouse
has won, won, won?

One has the MOST eggs.
One has the BIGGEST eggs.

One hasn't found an
egg—no, not one!

A sad little mouse,
wishing for an Easter egg,
runs away, feeling blue.

Sighing, spying,
trying to find an egg.
Looking, looking. What to do?

Stamp, tramp,
trip on a toadstool.

Stumble, tumble,
bump, bump, bump!

Down, down,
roll down the hill.

HERE is an Easter egg!
Jump, jump, jump!

27

Four Easter mice
dance in the spring-shine.

Dizzy, whizzy,
step, hop, bend.

Most eggs, biggest egg,
one has the BEST egg.

CRACK!   Surprise!

An Easter friend!